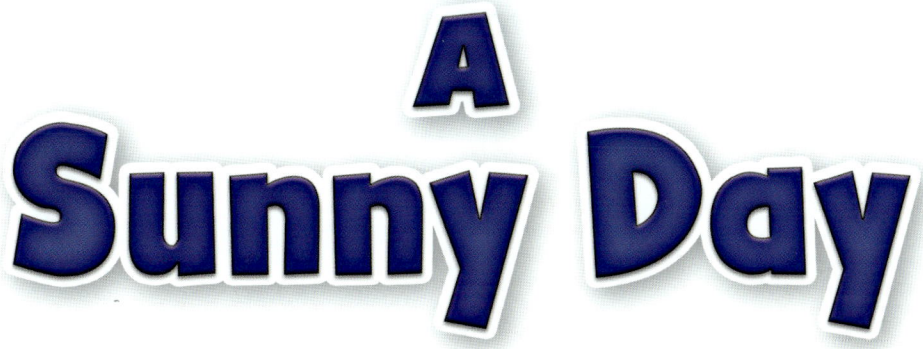

by Spencer Brinker

Consultant:
Beth Gambro
Reading Specialist
Yorkville, Illinois

Contents

A Sunny Day 2

Key Words 16

Index. 16

About the Author 16

New York, New York

A Sunny Day

Look!
It is sunny.

Today is sunny.

I see a blue sky.

Today is sunny.

I see a big ball.

Today is sunny.

I see an orange cat.

Today is sunny.

I see a small bug.

Key Words

ball   bug

cat   flower   sky

Index

ball 6–7   cat 8–9   sky 4–5
bug 10–11   flower 12–13

About the Author

Spencer Brinker lives and works in New York City. Weather never stops him from enjoying the city.